Mae and Marco's Space Journey

Written by Jim Al-Khalili and Raquel Pereira Crespo

Illustrated by Moreno

Contents

Collins

1 The force that holds space together

It's early afternoon on a bright, sunny day and adventurous friends, Mae and Marco, are waiting for a very rare event: a **total eclipse** of the Sun. Holding up special filters to protect their eyes when looking directly at the Sun, they discuss what is holding the Sun and Moon up in the sky. It's the **force** of **gravity** – which, strangely, is the same force that keeps us stuck on the ground. The quest for adventure bubbles up inside them.

"Let's build a rocket and go to the Moon!" says Mae.

Space scoop

The Moon is 400 times smaller than the Sun, but because it's also about 400 times closer to Earth, it looks the same size as the Sun to us.

2 How to defeat gravity

To build a rocket, Mae and Marco need to figure out how to overcome Earth's gravity. They have noticed that the harder they hit a tennis ball, the further it travels before it falls to the ground. What if you hit it so hard it never reaches the ground, but carries on falling *around* Earth? It's now in **orbit**. If you hit it any harder, it won't stay in orbit, but will fly off into space.

For a tennis ball to escape the pull of Earth's gravity, it would have to have a speed of over 40,000 kilometres per hour, or several times the speed of a bullet. This is called the "Earth **escape velocity**".

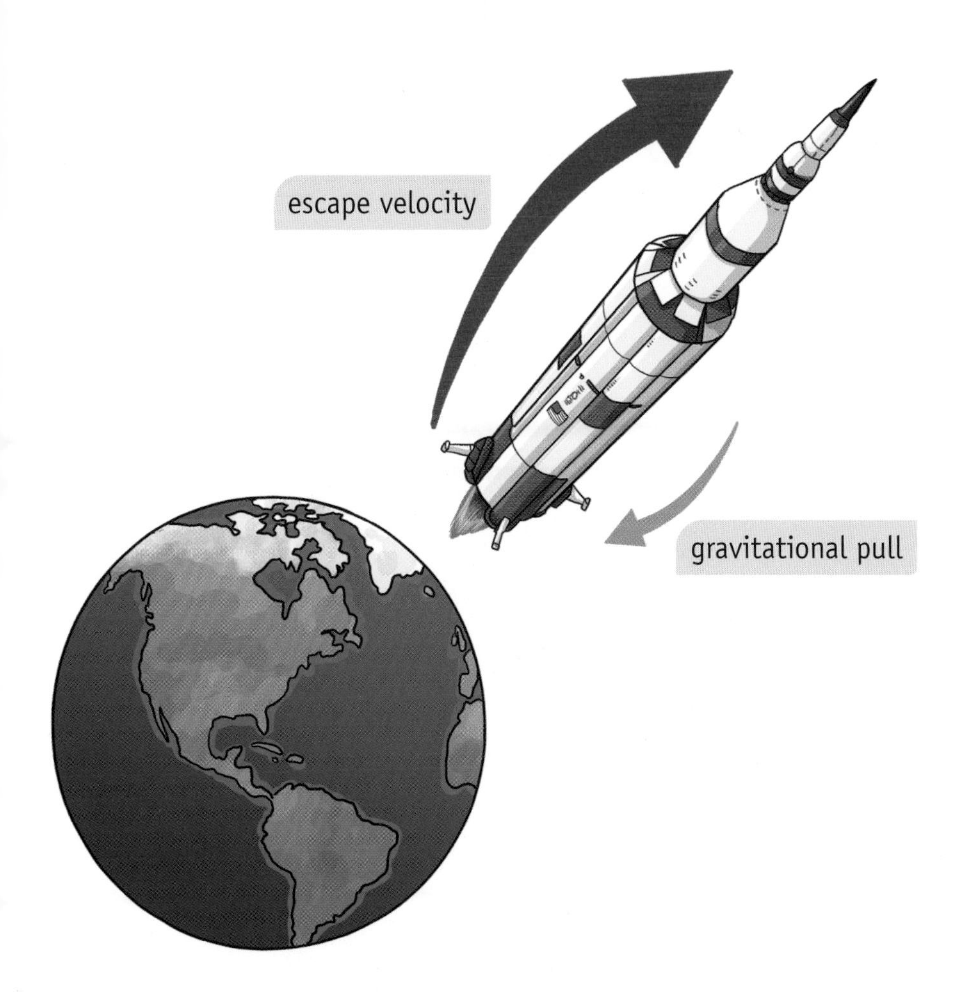

3 Rocket propulsion

Hitting a rocket with a giant tennis racket doesn't sound like a great idea. Instead, Mae and Marco's rocket will need to eject a great amount of hot, exploding gas so that it can be propelled upwards with enough force to send it into space.

Space scoop

The first rocket to leave Earth's **atmosphere** was the V2 missile which was launched by Germany during the Second World War in 1942.

4 The launch

Soon the big day arrives. Countdown begins: ten ... nine ... eight ... seven ... six ... five ... four ... three ... two ... one ...

Lift off! The rocket shakes and shudders as it slowly climbs upwards, but quickly picks up speed. Mae and Marco are squashed back into their seats as they **accelerate** upwards, just as you would be on a fairground ride.

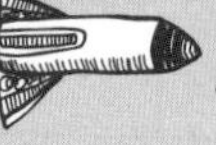

Space scoop

The first human to go into orbit was the **cosmonaut**, Yuri Gagarin, on 12th April 1961. He went all the way around Earth in his space capsule in 89 minutes.

Finally, it enters into orbit around Earth. This means that Mae and Marco's rocket engines can be turned off and they will float around Earth along with all the **satellites** – and, much further away, the Moon itself.

5 Disappearing gravity?

Marco releases himself from his seat and slowly floats upwards.

"Look Mae, I'm **weightless**. If I shut my eyes, it feels like I'm falling. It's very weird."

But where then does gravity go?

"The reason we feel weightless is because we're constantly in orbit around Earth," explains Mae. "If we stopped moving, we'd fall back to the ground."

Space scoop

When we say that something, like a satellite, is "in orbit" we mean that it is gripped by Earth's gravity like a ball on the end of a string that you swing around your head. The string that stops the ball flying off is like the pull of gravity.

6 Orbiting close to Earth

When in orbit, a day is very different because in 24 hours you will circle the Earth many times and get to see 16 sunrises and sunsets. During the day, Mae and Marco have a spectacular view of Earth with its thin layer of air. This is called the atmosphere and it protects life from the dangerous **radiation** that comes from space.

Space scoop

Earth is not the only planet with an atmosphere; most of the other planets in the Solar System, and even some of their moons, also have atmospheres, but ours is the only one that humans can breathe.

atmosphere

7 Amazing spacewalk

Mae and Marco are ready for their first spacewalk. Venturing outside their space capsule means they have to wear special spacesuits. These not only allow them to breathe in the **vacuum** of space, but protect them from extreme temperatures and dangerous radiation.

"We don't want to float off into space," Marco laughs nervously.

Mae, eager to go out, is the first to climb out of the hatch and let go.

Space scoop

When astronauts leave their spacecraft, it's called a "spacewalk", but a better name for it would be a "spacefloat".

8 Docking with the International Space Station

Today Mae and Marco are visiting the International Space Station (ISS for short). To get onto the ISS, they must approach it very carefully to avoid crashing into it, and attach their capsule to one of its entrances. This is called docking.

"Attachment beginning," announces their onboard computer.
It's a nervous few minutes.
Then, finally: "Firmly attached."
They hear cheering and applause from the astronauts on board the ISS on the other side of the dock.

Space scoop

The ISS orbits above the ground at an altitude of 400 kilometres and a speed of 30,000 kilometres per hour. This means it orbits all the way around Earth once every hour and a half.

a capsule docking on to the ISS

9 Seeking answers from experiments in space

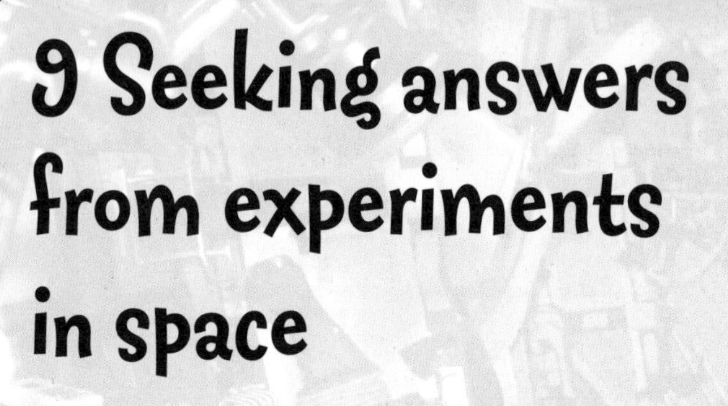

During their stay, Mae and Marco enjoy some free time and join in with the astronauts to carry out experiments in the weightless environment. Mae watches with delight as a few droplets of water escape from a bottle and combine into a single giant drop that floats in front of her face.

Space scoop

The International Space Station was launched at the end of the 20th century, which means for the whole of the 21st century so far, there have been humans in orbit around Earth (not the same ones, of course!) carrying out scientific experiments.

10 Space observatory fleet

After a couple of days on the ISS, it's time to leave. Back in their capsule, Mae and Marco detach from the ISS and fire their engines to head towards the Moon. They pass close by what looks like a large school bus.

Marco presses his face up to the window. "Look, Mae, that's the Hubble Space Telescope. It takes beautiful pictures of deep space and sends them back to scientists on Earth."

photos taken by Hubble

Space scoop

The James Webb Space Telescope will join Hubble and will be the biggest and most powerful space telescope ever launched into orbit. It might even find evidence of life on distant planets.

11 Our tiny home planet

After three more days, Mae and Marco approach the Moon. It looks huge up close and is covered in hundreds of bowl-shaped holes called craters.

They watch Earth emerge above the Moon's horizon.

Mae sighs. "Our home planet looks so beautiful and fragile from here, doesn't it? Hanging in the dark universe and hopelessly alone."

Space scoop

Earth formed with the rest of the **solar system** about five billion years ago.

12 Earth's Moon

As soon as they land on the Moon, Mae and Marco put on their spacesuits again. There is no atmosphere on the Moon, so they still need their oxygen tanks to breathe. Because the Moon is much smaller than Earth, its gravity is weaker and they feel much lighter.

This time, Marco is out first. He bounces down to the ground and back up again. "Look!" he exclaims. "I can jump six times higher than I can on Earth."

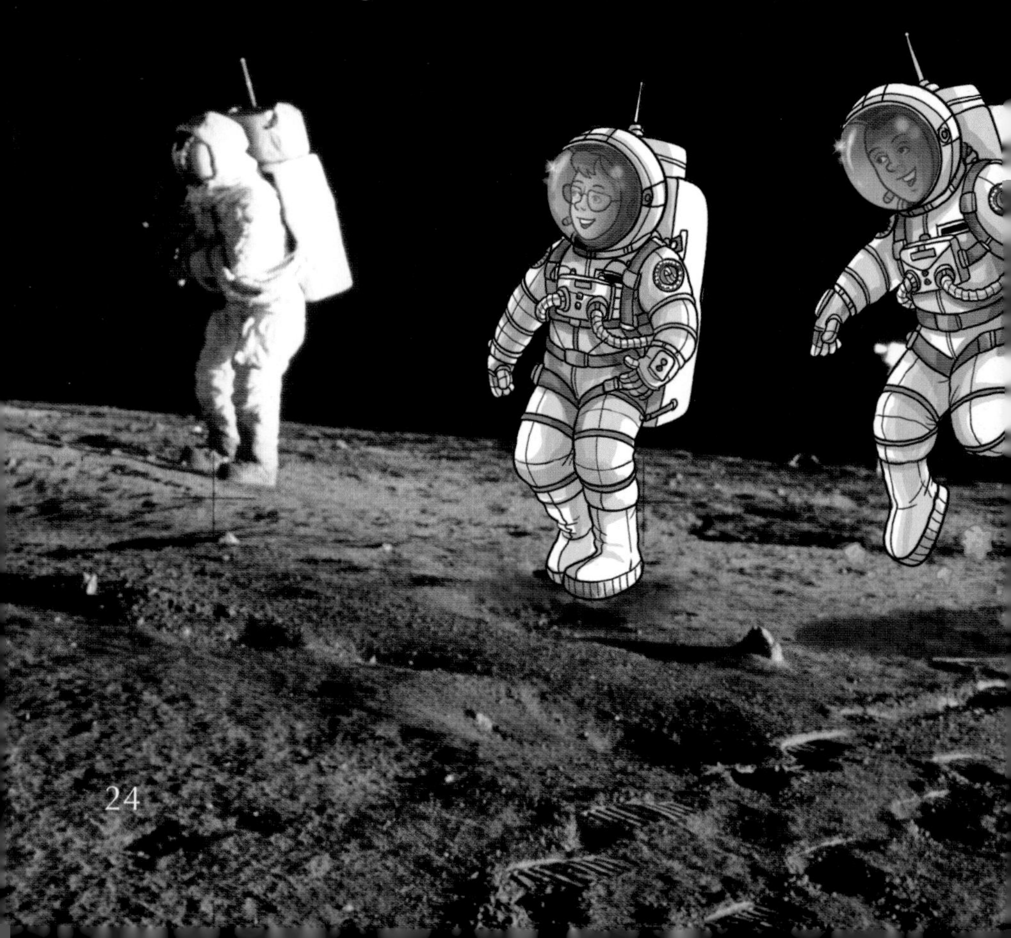

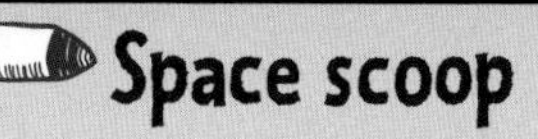

Space scoop

If you drop a hammer and a feather from the same height on the Moon, they will both land at the same time. The only reason the feather takes longer to fall on Earth is because there is air resistance. Since the Moon has no atmosphere, there's nothing to slow the feather down.

13 Heading home

After a few days of exploring the Moon and collecting rock samples, it's time to head back home. Mae and Marco's rocket doesn't need so much fuel to escape the Moon's weaker gravity and they're soon hurtling towards Earth again. Finally, the capsule's parachutes open and it lands softly on water, floating like a rubber duck in the bath.

"Well," says Marco, "I hadn't realised just how much there would be for us to see. Let's go to Mars next."

Mae laughs. "We're going to need a bigger rocket then!"

Space scoop

Since the first Moon landing in 1969, over 400 kilograms of rock samples from its surface have been brought back to Earth to study.

Glossary

accelerate speed up

atmosphere the air that surrounds the surface of a planet

cosmonaut a Russian Astronaut (or from the former Soviet Union)

escape velocity the speed needed for anything to escape the surface of a planet or moon and get into orbit around it

force the strength needed to make something move

gravity the force that pulls everything to the ground and keeps the Moon in orbit

orbit the route that is followed by the Moon and satellites as they move around the Earth

radiation another name for light or heat, but also means streams of tiny particles.

satellite any object or machine that is sent into orbit around the Earth

solar system our Sun and everything in orbit around it: all eight planets and their moons, as well as all other small objects

subatomic particles extremely tiny items smaller than atoms

total eclipse when the Moon moves across the Sun and blocks out its light entirely

ultraviolet light a type of invisible radiation, also called UV light for short

vacuum a space that contains no air or other gas

weightless having that floating feeling when gravity isn't pulling you downwards

Mae and Marco's space scrapbook

We built a rocket and flew to space.

Experiencing disappearing gravity – hey I'm weightless!

We did an amazing spacewalk.

Here we are in orbit above the Earth.

the International Space Station

walking on the Moon

Going home!

Ideas for reading

Written by Gill Matthews
Primary Literacy Consultant

Reading objectives:

- checking that the text makes sense to them, discussing their understanding and explaining the meaning of words in context
- identifying main ideas drawn from more than one paragraph and summarising these
- retrieve and record information from non-fiction

Spoken language objectives:

- maintain attention and participate actively in collaborative conversations, staying on topic and initiating and responding to comments
- participate in discussions, presentations, performances, role play, improvisations and debates

Curriculum links: Science – Light; Forces and magnets

Interest words: adventurous, rare, protect, quest

Resources: ICT

Build a context for reading

- Show children the front cover of the book and ask them to read the title. Explore children's ideas of what a space journey is. Establish children's existing knowledge of space and space travel.
- Ask children what sort of book they think this is. Read the back cover blurb and establish it is an information text.
- Ask what features children would expect to find in the book.

Understand and apply reading strategies

- Read p2 to give children the context of the book. Read the "Space scoop" box and check children's understanding of the facts.
- Ask why children think some of the words are in bold. Challenge them to find some of the words in the glossary and to read the definitions. If children are not familiar with glossaries, demonstrate how to do this.
- Read pp4–5 and model how to summarise the information on these two pages.